This
Treasure Cove Story
belongs to

OLAF'S FROZEN ADVENTURE

A CENTUM BOOK 978-1-912396-15-3
Published in Great Britain by Centum Books Ltd.
This edition published 2018. 1 3 5 7 9 10 8 6 4 2

Centum Books Ltd, 20 Devon Square, Newton Abbot,
Devon, TQ12 2HR, UK.

www.centumbooksltd.co.uk | books@centumbooksltd.co.uk
CENTUM BOOKS Limited Reg.No. 07641486.

A CIP catalogue record for this book is available
from the British Library.

Printed in China.

A Treasure Cove Story

Disney
Olaf's
FROZEN
ADVENTURE

Adapted by Andrea Posner-Sanchez
Illustrated by Joey Chou

There is a lot of activity in the Arendelle castle. Everyone is preparing for a holiday party.

'Surprise!' Olaf shouts as he jumps out from behind a pile of gifts.

'Not yet, Olaf,' Anna tells the little snowman.

'The surprise party starts *after* the Yule Bell rings,' Elsa reminds him.

Anna and Elsa are just as excited as Olaf.
It's their first Christmas together since they
were little girls!

'The first of many more to come,' Elsa
says, smiling at her sister.

They rush out to the courtyard to welcome all the townspeople. Kristoff and Sven are there to watch the ringing of the Yule Bell.

At exactly twelve o'clock, Elsa, Anna and Olaf ring the bell together. Then Elsa announces 'Let the holidays begin!'

Everyone cheers... and then turns to leave.
'Wait! Wait!' Anna calls after them.
'Won't you join us in the castle for a celebration?'
Elsa says.

'Thank you, Your Majesty,' says Mr Olsen,
'but we need to get home to knit socks for our
grandchildren. It's our family tradition.'
Everyone has their own traditions. No one
can stay for the party.

Kristoff tries to cheer up Elsa and Anna by showing them his holiday tradition. He plays a song and then reveals a rock statue of Flemmy the Fungus Troll.

'Now lick Flemmy's forehead and make a wish,' Kristoff says.

'Uh... no thank you,' the sisters say.

Olaf turns to Anna and Elsa. 'What's *your* family tradition?' he asks. 'Tell me!'

But because the sisters were apart for so many years, they don't have one.

'I'm sorry, Anna,' Elsa says sadly. 'It's my fault that we don't have a tradition.'

Olaf has an idea. He and Sven will find the
best holiday traditions and bring them back
to the castle for the sisters to enjoy.

The little snowman knocks on doors throughout the kingdom to ask the townspeople about their traditions. Some families make candy canes, some bake fruitcakes, some light candles and some decorate trees.

Soon Sven's sleigh is filled with holiday items
he has gathered. Olaf and Sven have just one more
house to visit.

'Hoo, hoo!' Oaken says when he sees them.
Oaken's family enjoys a steam bath for their holiday tradition. He gives Olaf a mini sauna, complete with hot coals. He puts it on top of Sven's sleigh.

But as Olaf and Sven head home, the sauna door opens and hot coals land on the other holiday items. Everything starts to burn.

Then the sleigh falls over a cliff! Olaf lands on one side of the gorge and Sven lands on the other.

'Okay, Sven,' calls Olaf. 'I'm not gonna sugarcoat it. This is a bit of a setback.'

Olaf still has one tradition left – A FRUITCAKE.

Meanwhile, Anna and Elsa are in the castle attic,
looking for any sign of their family traditions.
'I found my old Viking helmet and sorceress cloak
in my trunk,' Anna says. 'What's in yours, Elsa?'

'Mostly gloves,' Elsa replies as she looks through piles and piles of gloves. Then she gasps and pulls out a small box with bells on top. 'Maybe our tradition is in here...'

Olaf and Sven start to head home from opposite sides of the gorge. Sven's path is clear and easy. Olaf has to make his way through a dark forest filled with wolves!

'AWW, PUPPIES!' Olaf says excitedly.

Sven races to the castle stables to get help for his friend.

Sven finds Anna and Elsa and lets them know
that Olaf is in trouble.

'Oh, no!' Anna says. 'Olaf is lost in the forest?'

'And being chased by hungry wolves?' adds Elsa.

They quickly form a search party.

While searching in the woods, Anna notices a carrot poking out of a snowbank.

'Hmm. I wonder where Olaf could be,' she says.

'Well, he probably went on a mission to find traditions for Anna and Elsa,' a voice replies. 'But they caught fire and fell off a cliff. And then a hawk took the fruitcake.'

Sven gently grabs Olaf's carrot nose and pulls
him out of the snow.

'I'm sorry you still don't have a tradition,'
the snowman says sadly to Anna and Elsa.

'But we do,' Anna says as she opens the small box
from the attic. 'Look!'

Inside are drawings Anna made of Olaf when she
was a little girl.

The day Elsa created Olaf was Anna's fondest
memory. Every winter after that, Anna made
a drawing of Olaf as a holiday gift for her sister.

'You're the one who brought us together and kept us connected when we were apart,' Elsa explains. 'Olaf, *you're* our tradition.'

'SURPRISE!' shouts Anna.

Soon the townspeople make their way to the
forest clearing. They are relieved to see that Olaf
is safe. It's time to celebrate!

Elsa uses her magic powers to make
a beautiful ice tree. Children decorate
the tree with glowing lanterns.

'I think Arendelle has a new tradition,'
Elsa says happily.

Anna gives the snowman a warm hug.
'THANK YOU, OLAF!'